For Clemmie and Toby – my little muses.

Text and illustrations copyright © 2010 Rebecca Elliott
This edition copyright © 2010 Lion Hudson

The moral rights of the author
have been asserted

A Lion Children's Book
an imprint of
Lion Hudson plc
Wilkinson House, Jordan Hill Road,
Oxford OX2 8DR, England
www.lionhudson.com
Paperback ISBN 978 0 7459 6235 1
Hardback ISBN 978 0 7459 6267 2

First UK edition 2010
1 3 5 7 9 10 8 6 4 2
First US edition 2011
1 3 5 7 9 10 8 6 4 2 0

A catalogue record for this book is available
from the British Library

Typeset in 22/30 Garamond Premier Pro
Printed in China December 2010 (manufacturer LH06)

Distributed by:
UK: Marston Book Services Ltd, PO Box 269, Abingdon, Oxon OX14 4YN
USA: Trafalgar Square Publishing, 814 N Franklin Street, Chicago, IL 60610

Just Because

Rebecca Elliott

LION
CHILDREN'S

My big sister Clemmie
is my best friend.

She can't walk, talk,
move around much...

She's a lot like a princess.
They don't have to do much either.

They can just sit and look pretty.

Just because.

Some sisters can be mean.

They **scream** and shout,

pull your hair,

steal your chips,
and won't play cowboys
with you.

I don't know why they're
like that.

Just because.

Clemmie's not like that.

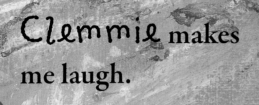

Clemmie makes
me laugh.

She makes sweet noises,

wears silly hats,

and pulls funny faces.

I don't know why these things
make me laugh.

Just because.

Clemmie helps me with my drawings.

She likes it when I draw pictures of trains, spoons, and dragonflies.

She doesn't like it when I draw pigeons.
I don't know why.

Just because.

We share a pet bug called **Simon.**

Clemmie likes him
because he *tickles* her hands.

I like him

just because.

Clemmie has a great chair.

Last week we went
to the moon on it.

I don't know why we didn't
go to Jupiter as well.

Just because.

Clemmie doesn't mind it
when I bang things really
LOUDLY

or chase the cat

or eat the crayons.

Sometimes I do these things

just because.

Clemmie has the BIGGEST curly hair
of anyone I know.

She doesn't like it being
brushed

or stroked

or braided.

She only likes it
being looked at.

Nobody knows why her
hair is so enormous.

Just because.

When it's really dark and there's thunder and lightning outside, I get really scared.

I don't know why.

Just because.

But Clemmie keeps very calm
and smiles because she likes the BIG NOISES.

This makes me feel
much better.

Before sleepytime she lets me look through her favourite books and point out my favourite pictures to her.

I'm good at pointing at things.
I don't know why.

Just because.

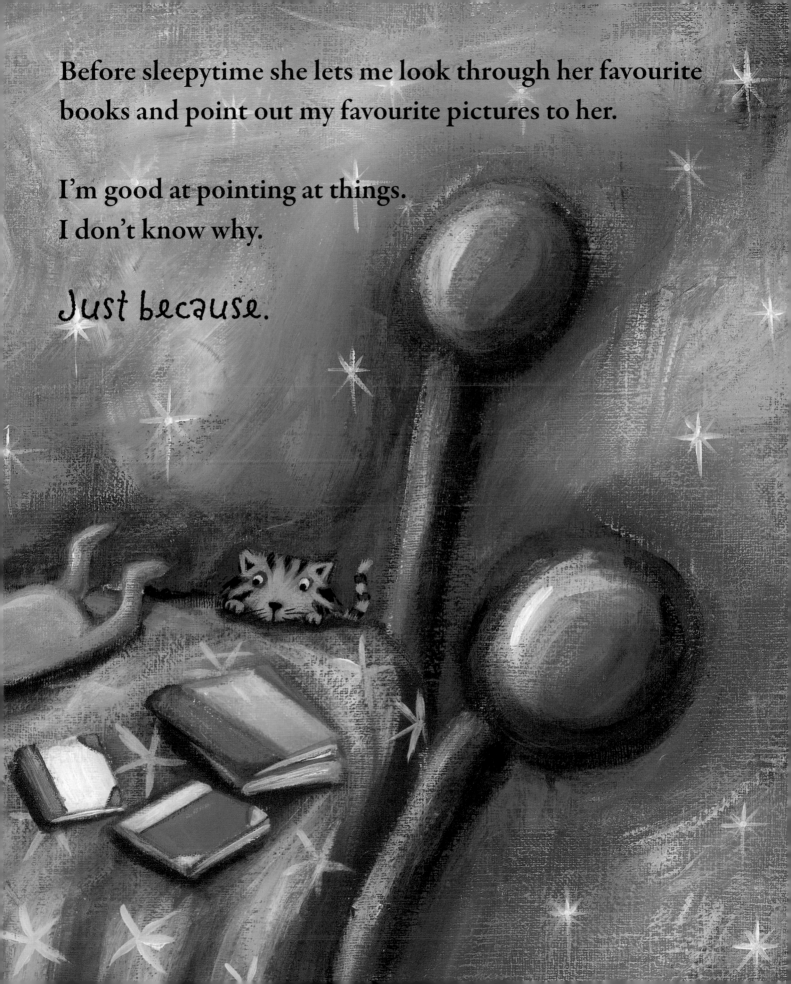

And when my eyes start to shut and I begin to dream of ice creams, tractors, and acorns, Clemmie just cuddles me really quietly and waits for me to go to sleep.

Clemmie's my best friend and I love her.
And I know exactly why.

Just because.